D0460676

Phaidon Press Inc.
180 Varick Street
New York, NY 10014

www.phaidon.com

English Edition © 2006 Phaidon Press Ltd
First published in French as *Marcellin Caillou* by Éditions Denoël
© 1969 Sempé and Éditions Denoël

ISBN-13: 978 0 7148 4714 6 (US edition)
ISBN-10: 0 7148 4714 3

A CIP catalogue record for this book is available from the British Library.

All rights reserved. No part of this publication may be reproduced, stored
in a retrieval system or transmitted, in any form, or by any means, electronic,
mechanical, photocopying, recording or otherwise, without the written
permission of Phaidon Press Limited.

Translated by Anthea Bell
Designed by Marianne Noble
Printed in China

Jean-Jacques Sempé

# M
artin Pebble could have been a happy little boy, like many other children.

But, *sad* to say ...

he had something that was rather unusual the matter with him:

he *kept* blushing.

He blushed at the least little thing,

or at nothing at all.

But luckily, you will say,

Martin wasn't the only child ever to blush. All children blush.

They blush when they are upset,

or when they do something silly.

But the thing about Martin

was the way he blushed for no reason.

It happened when he was least expecting it.

Although at times when he ought to have blushed,
he never blushed at all ...

In fact Martin Pebble had a very complicated life ...

He asked himself questions.

Or rather, one question ... always the same question:

*Why*
do
I
blush?

I could tell you that the Forest Fairy used her supernatural gifts on Martin, or I could say

that a clever doctor in a big modern city cured this interesting case.

But there were no local fairies,
   and, although there are a great many doctors in big modern cities,
      none of them was clever enough to cure Martin of blushing.

So

Martin

went

on

blushing,

**except, of course, at times when he really ought to have blushed ...**

*(all his friends are blushing at the mere idea that the same thing might happen to them, but Martin shows no emotion at all)*

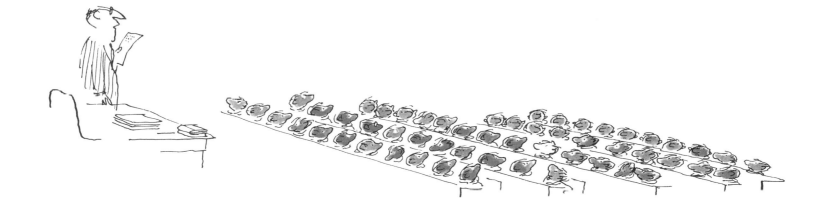

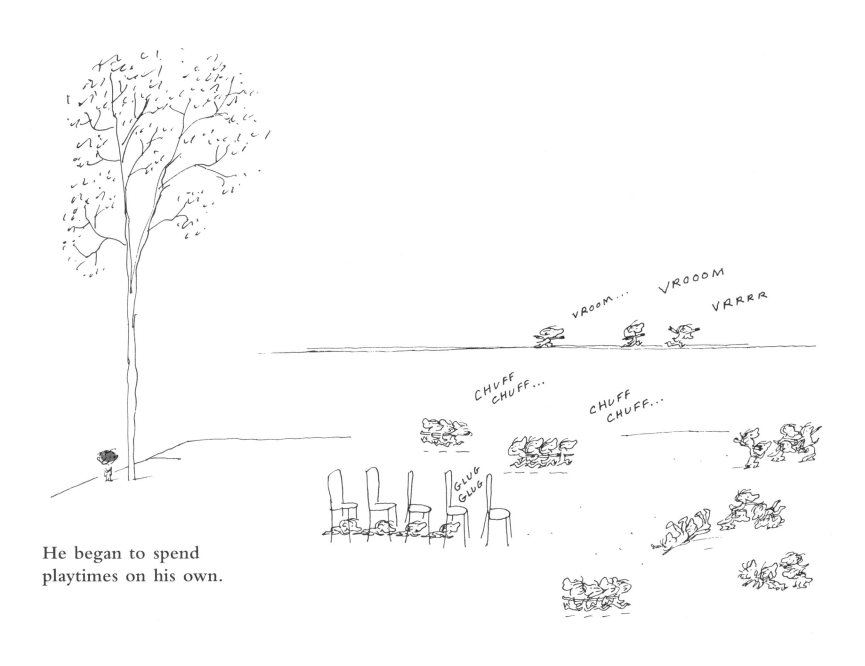

He began to spend
playtimes on his own.

He didn't play with his friends any more
when they were having fun with exciting games like cavalry charges,
or playing trains, planes and submarines.

This was because he hated hearing people make remarks about his complexion.

He preferred playing on his own.

I'm a bright red plane! I'm having so much fun!

He wished he was on vacation at the beach,
when at least other people were red too.

Because even in the middle of winter,

      when everyone was blue with cold,

            Martin was a very unusual color

                for the season.

He wasn't *very* unhappy, he just wondered how and why he blushed.

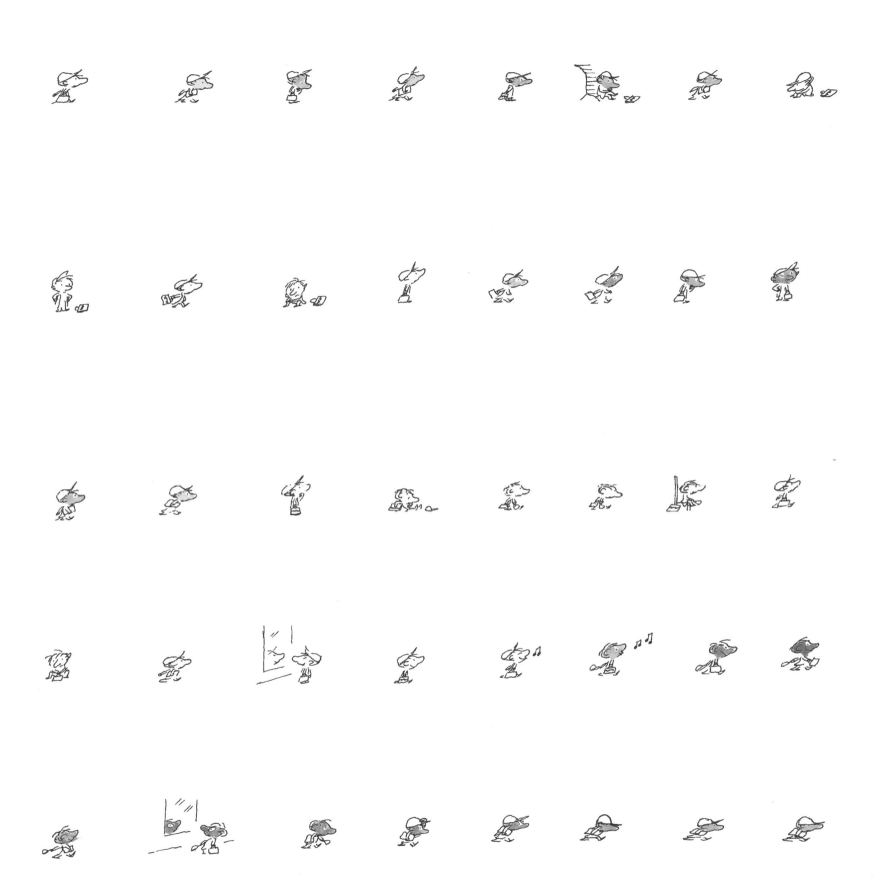

This question kept him awake at night.

One day, on his way home, blushing from time to time ...

as he was climbing up the stairs, he heard something like a sneeze ...

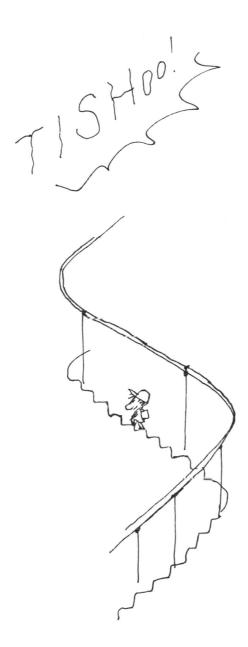

As he reached the second floor he heard another sneeze ...

and another on the third floor ...

Then he saw a boy on the fourth floor.

The boy was the person who had been sneezing so hard …

"You have a cold," said Martin.

It was his new neighbor, Roddy Rackett.

Little Roddy Rackett was a delightful child.
A brilliant violinist, good at schoolwork,
but since early childhood he had had something unusual the matter with him:

he sneezed a lot, even though he didn't have a cold ...

He told Martin that all this sneezing at the wrong
moment made life difficult for him.

For instance, he had sneezed when he was playing in a recital with grown-ups
at one of Madame Viviana's musical evenings,
which were very popular in the town of Little-Dreaming-on-Avon.

Everyone was talking about it,

and all Roddy Rackett could do was go for walks by himself beside the river, where the calm water and the sweet song of the birds were a comfort.

I'm not going to tell you that
the White Wizard of the River came along and cured him.
There were no local white wizards (and no local black wizards either).

And I'm not going to tell you that
a clever doctor in a big city gave him little pills that made him better.
No one cured him. No wizard ... and no clever doctor either.

He wasn't *very* unhappy.
It was just the way his nose tickled that bothered him.

Roddy noticed that Martin was blushing ...

They had a long talk.

That night they couldn't sleep a wink, they were so pleased to have met ...

They became inseparable.

Roddy played the violin for Martin.

And Martin,

    who was good at athletics,

        gave Roddy the technical advice an athlete needs

            if he is to make progress and avoid discouragement ...

As soon as Martin arrived anywhere he asked where Roddy was.

And wherever young Rackett went he was looking for young Pebble.

They played endless games of hide-and-seek on weekends and during vacations.

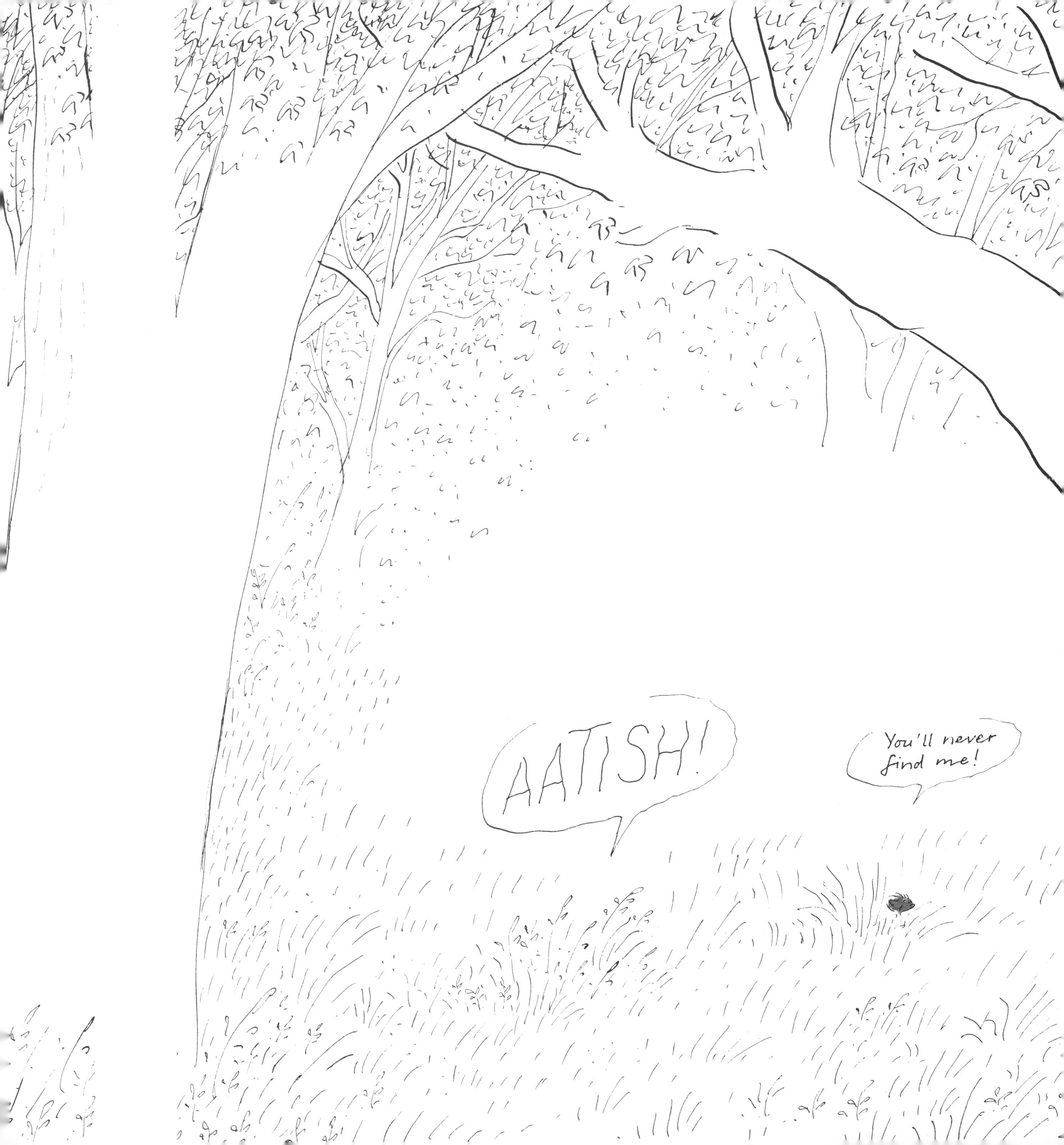
AATISH!
You'll never find me!

_AATISHOO!_

_ATISHOO!_

They had some very good times together.

On Speech Day at school,
Martin was delighted to see his friend
win applause for playing a lovely violin piece.

And Roddy was delighted
to hear the applause for Martin
when he recited a beautiful poem.

They were the best of friends.
 They played tricks on each other,

But they could just be together too, without talking,
because they were never bored in each other's company.

When Roddy had jaundice, Martin kept him company.
He was amazed to see just how yellow you can get ...

And when Martin had measles,
Roddy, who had already had it,
could see his friend whenever he wanted.

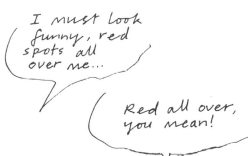

When Martin had a cold, he enjoyed sneezing like his friend.

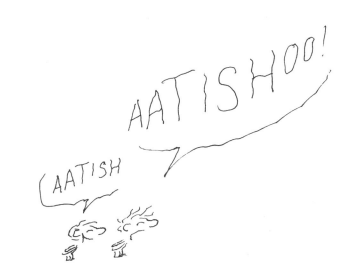

And when Roddy was sunburned one day he was happy to think
he could be as red as his friend ... sometimes.

They really were great friends.

# BUT

*(and those letters are rather black because what follows is rather sad)*

One day,

    when Martin was just home from his grandparents' house,

        where he had been spending a week of vacation,

            and his first thought was to go and find his friend Roddy,

he saw straw on the landing.

Someone he had never seen before opened the door.

He could see packing crates full of china ...

this time he blushed bright red in distress ...

The Rackett family had *moved* ...

He ran downstairs like a madman!

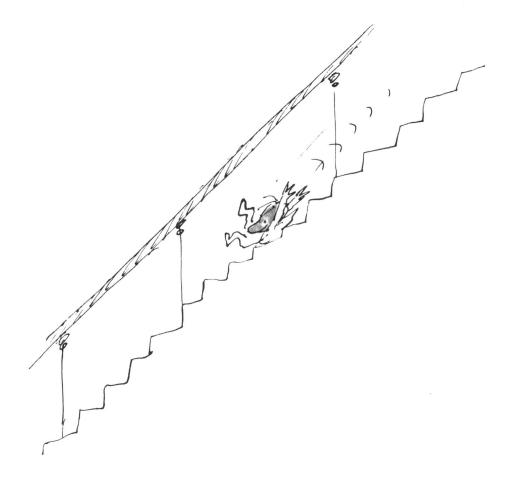

He even fell down the stairs,
from the third
to the second floor!

And he arrived home in tears.

But you know what parents are like.

        They're always so busy, rushed off their feet ...

The family spent a long time looking for Roddy's letter with his new address.

Days passed by, and Martin made other friends:

Patrick Cooper, who could whistle tunes through his fingers,

the Phillips brothers, twins with a passion for making things.
They'd make anything, and make it any which way.

*You'll never guess what she did to me...*

*Him too! Him too! What do you think he did to me?*

Paul Barker and his sister Katie,
who were always quarrelling,

*Don't worry, if anyone attacks you we'll look after you. You mustn't be scared!*

*That's right, you mustn't be scared. If anyone attacks you we'll be right here!*

Robert and Fred Leigh, two big-hearted
tough guys who were good at sports,

Ronald Bateman – he was a real laugh,
up to all sorts of tricks, wily as a fox.

not to mention Wayne Rowley,

a little redhead with glasses who was very absentminded.

Martin liked Wayne ...

because being absentminded made him so funny.

He hadn't forgotten Roddy Rackett.

He often thought about him,
and told himself he must find out what Roddy was doing now.

But when you're little, days go by and you never notice.

So do months ...

And so do years ...

Martin grew up.

He still blushed. Not so often, but he still blushed a bit.

Even when he was a grown-up gentleman.

A grown-up gentleman with telephones,

who took taxis,

and caught planes,

and rode in elevators.

He lived in a big city where everyone was in a hurry,

and he was in a hurry just like everyone else ...

One day when he was standing in the rain waiting for a bus,
feeling very stressed because he had meetings ...

with Mr. Larch at 9.15,
Mr. Parfitt at 9.45,
Mr. Ribble at 10.15,
Mr. Burleigh at 10.45,
Mrs. Brownsmith at 11.15,
and Mr. Percival at 11.45,

he heard someone with a cold, sneezing so hard
that Martin began laughing, like everyone else.

He looked at the man with the cold ...

 *(I don't need to explain why these letters are pink ...)*

It was Roddy Rackett!!

I did try,
        but I couldn't possibly describe the joy
        of the two friends when they met again!

Roddy Rackett was a violin teacher now.

They exchanged all their news.

At his friend's request, Roddy played the violin.

As for Martin, he showed that he was as good at athletics as in his youth.

They even ran a race,

which Martin only just won.

And indulged in silly games that serious people might think odd in two grown men.

They spent a happy afternoon together, making plans.

If I wanted to make you sad,
I would tell you that the two friends,
with so much to do now that they were grown up,
never met again.

And in fact they didn't meet most of the time.
You find an old friend. You're overjoyed. You make plans.
And then you lose touch.

Because you're short of time, you have too much work,
the two of you live too far apart.

And for lots of other reasons.

But Martin and Roddy *did* meet again.

In fact they often met again.

Whenever Martin went anywhere, he immediately asked if Roddy was there.

And Roddy Rackett could always find Martin Pebble.

They went out on long hunting expeditions
(and never caught anything).

AATISH.

They played silly games.

But they could ...

also sit quietly,

talking or not talking,

By the way, have you noticed? My elder son Robert... I don't know what the matter is, but he sneezes a bit for no reason... he sneezes quite a lot really... It's odd...

Yes, it's certainly odd. I wonder where he gets it from? It's like my boy Michael, now and then he blushes red... really scarlet! Very odd!

because they were never bored in each other's company.

CATISHOO!

Sempé . 1968-69.